I0788483

Gus Finds A Way

By Linda Nelson

Copyright © 2023 Linda Nelson

Published in 2023 by Book Writing Founders
www.Bookwritingfounders.com

This Book Is Dedicated To My Grandchildren

Taylor, Joseph, Holden, Ava, and Austin
whom I love very much

The campus was as active as ever, with students everywhere on the first day of classes. Gus especially loved this day because there was always a lot of food around, and everyone was in a good mood.

As he was moving around the campus, he noticed there seemed to be more squirrels than he had ever seen before. That was odd because he knew all the squirrels by their faces, even if he did not know them by name.

Why so many squirrels? He wondered. *What was attracting them to this campus today?* He decided to call a meeting with Clyde, Rocky, Freddie, and Patty and see if they knew anything about the increase in squirrels. He was able to find Clyde by the fountain looking for lizards but no one else. He asked Clyde about all the squirrels but Clyde was not interested in Gus' curiosity and just said he did not notice more squirrels than usual. Gus moved onward.

He came across a new squirrel named Baxter.

Baxter told him that he traveled to get to the campus for many days to escape being caught by the animal squad. Gus could not believe what he was hearing.

Baxter

An animal squad and a NET; this was not good. He asked Baxter to tell him all about it. Baxter told Gus the squirrels were destroying property at campuses and parks, and even at some private properties. Gus could not believe such a thing was happening. Squirrels are peaceful animals and would not hurt anyone. They mostly gather nuts and simply enjoy being together.

Baxter said that the man in the car with the net comes at night and tries to capture as many squirrels as possible. Then he takes them to other locations where there are less squirrels, and he can keep them under control.

Gus was not believing what he was hearing. What would happen if his friends and Patty were captured and taken away? What would he do and how would he know where they were taken and how could he get them back? Gus was so scared to tell his friends. How would they protect themselves from this terrible man and net?

Gus thought, first things first. He was going to have to tell the squirrels just what he found out and come up with a plan. He searched the campus but still could not find anyone. He thought that was strange. Patty was not at home and where were Clyde, Freddie, and Rocky? After many hours of searching, Gus just went home feeling scared and sad about the news from Baxter.

The next day was sunny and warm. Gus left his tree in search for the others. He stopped by Patty first, and she was not home. Could she have told him she was leaving for a few days and he forgot? The others were nowhere to be found either.

Now he was really beginning to get worried, maybe the man with the net found them and took them. What a terrible thought.

He calmed down a bit when he saw Joy and Hero. They were sitting under his tree. He went to them and started jumping up and down to make sure they noticed he was there. Hero started barking, and Joy knew Gus was there. Gus started to communicate to them as only he could what he had heard from Baxter. They could not believe what he said. How could they help find Patty and the others?

Gus did not have an answer yet, but he thanked them and told them he was going to look around campus again. Maybe they were in the cafeteria; he had not checked there.

When Gus reached the cafeteria, the squirrels were not there. In fact, they were not at their usual play places or at home. This puzzled him.

He went to his tree and just stayed there for a bit. All of a sudden, Patty appeared. He ran down the tree so quickly that he fell on his head. He grabbed Patty and hugged her he was so glad to see her. She stopped him and told him she and the other squirrels were in hiding.

"Why?" He asked her, surprised. She told him that there was a man with a net looking for squirrels to take away. He could not believe she knew about the NET. What Baxter had told him was really true and happening right now. Gus told her about Baxter and that he had been searching for them and her for days and was so worried.

Patty took Gus to the hiding place. He was so glad to see Clyde, Freddie, and Rocky. They danced around for a bit then sat down to think about a way they could be safe from the man with the net. This was going to take a long time, and lots of thought and safe hiding if they were going to stay on campus. Who could they turn to for help? Hero and Joy were willing to help — that was a start.

They stayed in the new hiding place: a big old oak tree with just enough room to fit through the hole. They tried to come up with a plan.

One day while Gus was out, he met one of the students. The students asked him, where were all the squirrels? Gus was surprised by this comment. He was not quite sure how to answer. If he said they were all still there, then the student might tell other students, and they would risk being caught. He decided to say nothing.

A few days later, Gus met the same student and he asked the same question again. This time Gus gave him the answer. The student was shocked by his response. He told Gus that he will let the students know what was happening and come up with a plan. Gus was still not sure if he did the right thing telling the student, but he knew most students, and they were good friends.

Gus and Patty decided to go out one evening to get something from Patty's home. They were very careful as the man with the net usually came in the evening. They made it to her house and back without being seen. They decided they would not try that again.

A few days later, the student saw Gus and asked him if all the squirrels could come to a meeting as he might have a plan for them. Gus was so excited to hear this that he could not run fast enough to tell the others. When he arrived and told Patty about what the student had asked him to do, she immediately rounded up all the squirrels.

The students presented their idea. It was a very simple one; why had no one thought about it? The students loved seeing the squirrel's and loved each one of them, and did not want them to be taken away. The idea was to have all the campus squirrels wear a blue ribbon around their neck. Those without the ribbon would have to go. What a brilliant idea!

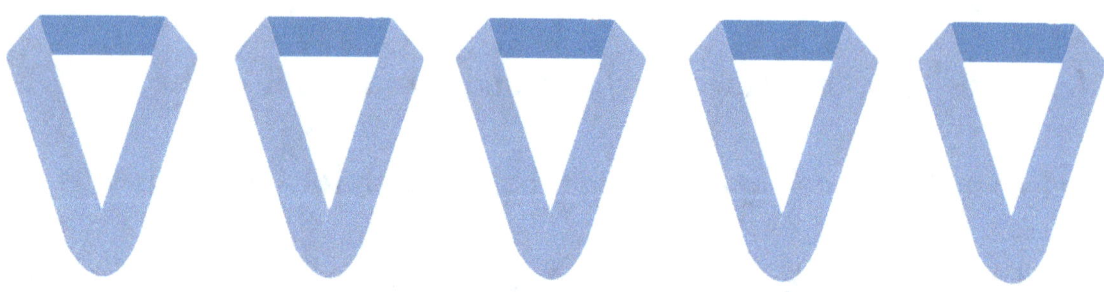

Everyone would have a home, no one would be taken away, and they could control the number of squirrels. There would be enough food and shelter for everyone. The students told the squirrels that the man with the net thought it was a great idea. "Now we have to round up all the squirrels and get blue ribbons on them." The students announced. This was not going to be an easy task, but Gus was determined to save the squirrels on HIS campus.

He quickly ran to see if he could find Joy and Hero and tell them the plan.

Maybe they would want to help as Joy had mentioned to him. He checked

his tree as quickly as possible but they were not there.

He checked the cafeteria, and no luck. He could not spend any more time

doing this as it was getting late and he would possibly be caught by the

man with the net.

Unable to find Joy and Hero, he returned to the squirrels' hiding place.

They were all safe there.

The next morning, Gus tried again to find Joy and Hero, this time he

found them. They were just coming from classes. Gus told Joy and Hero

about the plan, and they were more than ready to help. Joy said she

would pick up the ribbons and give them to the other students. Gus would

then round up all the squirrels, and the ribbons would be put on them.

Gus quickly ran to the hiding place. He told the squirrels to count how

many ribbons they would need and get back to him so he could tell Joy.

Everyone was so excited that they kept falling over each other and running in different directions until Gus said STOP, and then order was achieved.

When all the squirrels were together again, Freddie asked, why the color BLUE was chosen? Gus thought about that for a minute. Then said, "remember when I was BLUE and you all painted yourselves with different colors so I would not feel different? Well, now we are and always will be together so BLUE will always be our color."

It seems that each campus squirrel will have a different color. No one will ever get lost and everyone can come to each campus and be with friends anytime they want. They will know where their home is. Everyone liked that idea. It made everyone feel safe to know they were loved and protected.

The day finally arrived when they would be getting their BLUE ribbons. Everyone was excited. The students gathered by the fountain to see this special day. Everyone would remember this forever.

Who would go first? This was a really hard decision.

There had to be a vote.

The students and squirrels all had to vote.

When everyone had voted, Joy and Hero were elected to pull the name of

the first squirrel to get the blue ribbon.

It was Patty.

Everyone was so happy, especially Gus. Now, all the squirrels took their turn getting ribbons and they looked great. Finally, everyone would be safe from the man with the net. He was no longer an enemy. He was a friend who would always be there, taking them to safety if they needed it. No getting lost, no more nets, just friends helping friends. How wonderful.

Baxter found Gus and told him how wonderful having a BLUE ribbon was and that they would be friends always. Gus was happy knowing Baxter thought of him as his friend now that he would always be safe.

He thought about how lucky he was to have such good friends and the students who really helped keep them safe. Especially, Joy and Hero; he would really miss them when Joy graduated this year. He decided to try and find them, and tell them just how special they really are. He went by his tree and just as he had hoped they were there.

Joy felt the ribbon on Gus, and Hero barked with pleasure. What a great feeling to have special friends that care about you and are so glad you are safe. Gus told Joy and Hero how much he would miss them after graduation. Joy told them they would come back and visit whenever they could. This made Gus elated and excited.

Everyone was taking photos of the squirrels with their ribbons on, and Joy was going to have the photo placed in the yearbook.

Gus was speechless when Joy told him that and started to run around the tree. Since the squirrels did not have to hide anymore, Gus went to find Clyde, Freddie, Rocky, and Patty to tell them what Joy had said. They would not believe it either but were so happy to now have a lasting memory.

Gus thought the squirrels should give a gift to Joy and Hero for graduation. What could it be? It has to be something so special that they would always think of them when they looked at it. Gus said this is your homework to think of a gift for Joy and Hero. The squirrels had a real assignment from Gus this time.

After many, many suggestions, the squirrels finally came up with what they hoped would be the perfect gift. It was to be a medal with a blue ribbon on it. Everyone loved the idea. Gus was put in charge of having it made, and everyone would have to be present to give it to Joy and Hero at graduation. Everyone agreed.

Finally, it was graduation day, the squirrels were so excited. Gus found Joy and Hero in the mass of students. It was hard not to get stepped on but he managed. He told Joy and Hero he wanted to say goodbye but needed all the squirrels to be here with them. So they walked over to Gus' tree where all the other squirrels were eagerly waiting. They chirped and squealed so that Joy and Hero could hear them.

Gus said, "we had this Braille medal made especially for you and Hero to thank you for everything you did for us and for just being our friend. We love you." Hero started barking

and barking and wagging his tail, and Joy could not keep from crying. Her tears fell on Gus, and he started to cry along with her. It was so beautiful.

Joy said this was not goodbye but a friendship that would never end. Gus turned to Clyde, Freddie, Rocky, Patty, and Baxter and said that was the best news I heard all day.

Friendship, by definition, is a mutual trust of a person or persons. To those who are fortunate to have such a person in their lives, treat them as a gift and cherish them always.

The End

About the Author

Linda Nelson lives on the East End of Long Island, New York, and is a graduate of Chamberlayne College in Massachusetts. She has written articles about animals and their behavior in a fictional form for some time. Her inspiration for this book was her love of children and the pleasure that reading brings to a young audience. This Blue Squirrel brings you directly into the adventures of its main character Gus whom you would learn to admire and want to read more about.

Presently, another sequel is being worked on and hope to be completed by year's end.

... More to read from Linda Nelson
Find it on Amazon